Out of Season

Bob Stone

Part of
SEASONS OF LOVE
Anthology

Beaten Track
www.beatentrackpublishing.com

Out of Season

First published 2018 by Beaten Track Publishing
Copyright © 2018 Bob Stone

ISBN: 978 1 78645 247 4

Cover Design: Trevor Howarth

Beaten Track Publishing,
Burscough. Lancashire.
www.beatentrackpublishing.com

Dedication

For Wendy, my love every season.

Contents

1.

REMICK HAD WALKED the worlds for millennia, keeping only his own company. Time belonged to him, and he was content to go where and when he pleased or was needed, his life solitary and unending. The possibility that he might be lonely had never occurred to him until the day he saw the woman in the coffee shop. He had been called many things in his time. He and his kind had been called demons, the Old Ones, even gods, but never anything as mundane as lonely.

His day had, up until that point, been fairly routine. He had secured the temporal bonds between two worlds which had become frayed and brittle. There had been a small amount of leakage, but the only witness had been a teenage girl who became convinced she had seen a ghost. She was, however, prone to telling her friends tall stories and realised that if she mentioned the old woman who had drifted into her room and out through the wall, nobody would believe her, so she said nothing.

Once the temporal bonds had been secured, Remick moved on to quell an uprising in a time that had yet to happen. Because he still had a great deal to do, he found that the best way was to remove the leader of the uprising from the time-stream altogether. With their leader gone, his followers found they no longer had any interest in the uprising and went home. The morning's work done, Remick had an irresistible urge for a double-shot hazelnut latte. What he actually wanted was a beer, but it was too early in most of his days for beer, so a latte would have to do.

He was doing his best to enjoy his drink, even though the barista had used rather too much syrup, making the latte overly sweet. At least there was one of those little biscuits with the coffee, and he did enjoy those. Outside, grey rain was steadily pouring down, as it had been doing for days. Winter had just started, and spring was a long way away, but the coffee was warm.

While Remick was drinking, his attention was caught by a man and a woman at a nearby table. The woman was quite simply the most breathtakingly, heartbreakingly beautiful person he had ever seen. He had seen, admired—and sometimes acted upon—beauty in many women and men in his travels, but never had he encountered anyone quite as fascinating as this.

It was not her hair, though it was black as carbon just before it starts to become diamond. She had been wearing a woollen hat when she arrived, but her hair, once free of it, cascaded over her shoulders, providing a stark contrast to her red coat.

It was not her skin, which had a texture that he felt he could never tire of touching, even though it was only the skin of her lovely face that was visible. It was not her eyes, which were as dark as midnight and sparkled with constellations of mischief. It was none of these things and yet all of them.

What was most striking was that he could not read her future timeline. She was an enigma, her destiny unknowable. The man with her was taking no notice of her astonishing beauty, just talking about himself and occasionally looking at his phone. The woman was a rare and priceless treasure; the man was a priceless idiot.

Remick continued to stare at the woman. She was talking to the man, telling him a charming story about something that had happened to a someone named Helen in the department store where she worked. She made the story entertaining, imitating several different voices, but still the man paid her only perfunctory attention, giving the occasional grunt or *mmm* to give the impression he was listening, when anyone could see he was not.

Remick found the woman's persistence in trying to gain her companion's interest at once delightful, because she was trying so hard, and upsetting because it was not working. He knew that he could listen to her stories and look at her face as she was telling them for a very long time indeed without ever tiring, and if there was something about which Remick knew a great deal, it was long times. It was at that moment, that one, glorious moment that stretched out for what felt like hours, that Remick knew he was lonely, and his loneliness could only be remedied by having this woman in his life. Remick carried on watching until the woman finished her tale, and the man said something about having to get back to the office.

As he drained his now cooling coffee, Remick watched the couple get up and leave. They seemed to be together, and yet there was little connection between them. The man opened the door but was oblivious to whether the woman had even followed him out. They rushed past the coffee shop window through the rain and out of sight, and there and then, Remick made a decision. He would have another latte and come up with a plan.

2.

THE PLAN WAS a fairly straightforward one, and the opportunity to put it into action arose three days later. During those three frustrating days, Remick had spent so much time in the coffee shop he had been given a loyalty card and had almost acquired enough stamps to get a free cup of coffee.

For the first two days, he watched and he waited, but neither of the pair came in. It was tedious, but at least it gave Remick shelter from the rain, which was showing no sign of letting up and was now accompanied by a fierce, chilly wind. On the afternoon of the third day, his patience was rewarded when the man came in and ordered a large Americano with no milk and a raisin Danish. He went and sat at a table by the window and became immersed in something on his phone. He did not appear to be expecting company.

Remick had known the man would be there, of course. His timeline had been transparent and predictable. It was the unreadable woman who had made Remick return to the coffee shop every day and consume too many lattes. It was not because he wanted to see her, though he most certainly did; it was that he wanted to catch the man on his own.

Remick, confident that he had not been observed, bought himself yet another latte and went over to the table where the man sat, typing something into his phone and smiling in the way of someone greatly amused by their own humour. Remick indicated a chair at the other side of the table and enquired, "Is anyone sitting here?"

The man looked up from his phone, looked at Remick, looked at the chair, and finally looked around at all the other vacant chairs in the coffee shop. He was obviously unwilling to be seen sharing a table with this stranger, with his unkempt beard and long hair which could do with a wash. And a cut.

"There are loads of free chairs," he said.

"I know," Remick replied. "But I like the look of this one."

The man sighed and waved a hand vaguely at the chair. Then he turned his body towards the window and away from Remick. *Sit there if you want,* the gesture said, *but don't expect me to talk to you.* Remick found it incredibly rude, and it made him even more determined to carry out his plan.

"Have you got the time?" he asked.

The man glanced at his watch. "Ten to," he said, then went back to his texting.

"No, you misunderstand me. I know what time it is. I always know what the time is. It's a gift. And it's actually eight minutes to. I meant have you got the time? I was wondering if you have got the time left in your life to waste it with someone who does not interest you in the slightest."

The man looked up and stared at Remick, his face a mixture of confusion and irritation. "Look, I don't know who you think you are, but—"

"I don't *think* I'm anyone," Remick replied, interrupting him. "I know who I am. I know who you are, too. It *is* Brian, isn't it? Brian Norris?"

"Who are you?" the man demanded. "Are you from the VAT, because—"

"No, Brian. I'm not from the VAT. They won't be visiting you unexpectedly until next Thursday, I believe. How you fiddle your VAT returns is of absolutely no concern to me. It also may not be relevant to you, but that depends on what you do with the suggestion I am about to make."

Norris stood up, making a great show of finishing his coffee.

"Look, I don't know what you want, but I'm really busy. I've got a business to run, so I suggest you sod off and go and bother someone else."

"Sit down, Brian," Remick said pleasantly. When Norris remained on his feet, he said it again, and this time it could not be described as pleasant. "Sit *down*!"

Norris glared at Remick, but mutely sat back down.

"That's better." Remick smiled again. "It's always best to keep things polite."

"What do you want?" Norris hissed, glancing around in case there was anyone else in the coffee shop who might know him.

"It's really very simple. The woman you were with in here the other day. I want you to end things with her."

"Which woman? I don't know what—"

"Oh don't be ridiculous, Brian. You know very well who I mean. I don't really think that a man like you would have many women. She's very beautiful, and you are completely unworthy of her, so you will end it. Today."

This incensed Norris, and he leaned forward in his chair, pushing his face up close to Remick's. He smelled of cheap aftershave and cheaper cigarettes.

"Now you listen," he snarled, his mouth a thin, angry line. "She's got nothing to do with you. I'm not used to being threatened, so either you back off right now, or...well, let's just say I know people."

"You know people?" Remick laughed. "What a curious expression. Of course you know people. Most people know other people. The thing is, most of the people you know dislike you. They think you are a self-obsessed, arrogant idiot. And of course, they're right. You are."

Norris did not seem to have a ready reply to this. He sat back in his chair, folded his arms across his chest and stared at Remick.

"So," Remick continued, "here's my offer to you. If you end your relationship, such as it is, with that woman today, by, say, five o'clock, I will leave you alone. You will never see me again and you will continue with your rather miserable existence. Your life will carry on exactly as it is now. You will run your business badly until your creditors catch up with you in about two years time and force you to sell up. You will go on thinking you are happier than you actually are and die reasonably peacefully in your bed in twenty-eight years time. If you don't, however…"

"What? What if I don't?"

"Then your life will end twenty-eight years earlier than it was supposed to, and it won't be very peaceful, I'm afraid."

Norris stood up again, shoving his chair back so violently it almost toppled over.

"That's it!" he declared. "I've had enough. You can't come here and threaten me like this!"

"Five o'clock," Remick said with a slight smile because he now knew what he would be doing at that time.

He watched Norris storm out of the coffee shop and then went and ordered himself another latte. Because he was in a good mood, he treated himself to a slice of lemon drizzle cake to go with it.

3.

At five o'clock, Remick was waiting outside the office block where Brian Norris rented a suite of rooms for his web design business. He sat on a bench on a small patch of grass at the front of the office block. The rain had stopped for a while, but the wind was still strong, whipping old newspapers and takeaway coffee cups around his feet. The bench was surrounded by discarded cigarette butts, despite the very clear notice next to the bench politely requesting smokers use the bin nearby. There were times, Remick thought, when the human race did not deserve the world that had been provided for them.

Remick was dressed innocuously in a long, black leather coat and jeans, his normal attire for walking in this world. Although he had made frequent studies of the clothing and habits of the people in every time period he visited, he had not chosen his outfit out of any desire to fit in. He just liked the way it looked. He sat pretending to be interested in a copy of the local newspaper which he had found on the bench and was several days out of date. He was not really reading the news; he knew only too well what today's news was and tomorrow's as well, and the wind made it hard to keep the paper still. He waited until his internal clock ticked round to five o'clock and watched as Brian Norris emerged from the building.

Norris was worried about something, if the frown etched into his brow was any indication. He walked hurriedly, looking all around him with anxious eyes, the collar of his coat turned up, ostensibly against the wind but really intended to obscure his face, as if that would make any difference. Because he was looking around, he very nearly walked straight into Remick, who had risen from the bench as Norris approached and stood right in front of him.

"Hello, Brian," he said. "Don't try and run. You won't be able to."

Norris was not used to being told what to do, Remick could tell. He watched in amusement as the human stubbornly tried to move but found that his legs would not cooperate. All around him, people passed by, rushing home from work and oblivious to his plight. It was almost as if they were not there at all. The air was still, and he could no longer feel the wind. He wanted to ask Remick what was about to happen to him but found that his mouth did not work any better than his legs.

"You had a chance to do the right thing, Brian," Remick said. "One chance. It wasn't even as if it was a difficult thing to do, but I knew you wouldn't do it. Your sort never do. So here's what I have done. I've taken you out of time. But because you're not really a bad person, just vain and arrogant, you're not going to die. I could end your existence without thinking about it and without regret, but instead, I'm just going to leave you here. It will give you plenty of time to have a good old think about how you could have done things differently."

As he spoke, Remick's eyes flashed red with a fire that burned into Norris's mind and soul, and then suddenly Remick and the familiar background of the world he knew were gone, leaving Norris alone and cold and screaming in a vast, empty, timeless void.

People carried on with their lives, scurrying along to catch trains or buses, phones clamped to their ears, having meaningless conversations that could easily have waited until they got home. The wind continued to blow litter in circles like small animals playing chase. The world could, and would, continue to thrive without Brian Norris and his web-design business. Remick grinned. That was the easy part of his plan completed.

4.

THE NEXT PART of Remick's plan required him to be patient again. He knew it would be fruitless to return to the coffee shop immediately, so busied himself with other things. A girl had been born on all the worlds, and Remick knew that, like her brother, one of her would one day be important. Remick spent a little time investigating, and once he was satisfied he knew which version of the girl was the important one, he returned to the world with the coffee shop and the woman.

The rain had also returned. The skies were heavy and the colour of old slate. Remick waited across the road from the coffee shop, pretending to look in a shop window. When he saw the woman approach, it should have been like a small patch of spring had arrived, but in her dark-grey coat and the hat she had been wearing when Remick first saw her, she looked as downcast as the weather. Remick felt a little sad for her, but it was all part of his plan, and he fully expected her mood would change soon. He waited until he was sure she had entered the coffee shop and gave her time to order her drink, then crossed the road and followed her.

The coffee shop windows had misted up, so it was not until he had gone inside that he spotted her. She was sitting on her own in a corner booth, her gloveless hands wrapped around a steaming mug to warm them. Enchanted by her long, slender, ringless fingers, Remick forced his gaze to the phone beside her at which she kept casting glances, as if she could not quite believe there had been no messages since the last time she looked—mere seconds ago.

Remick ordered himself a latte—no syrup this time, he was starting to find the taste cloying—and sat at the nearest free table. From his coat pocket, he pulled a battered paperback copy of Proust's *A La Recherche de Temps Perdue* in the original French and opened it at a random page. He was not reading it—he found Proust's prose stodgy, the language over-elaborate—but he had carefully selected the paperback from the shelves of a charity shop because it seemed appropriate and he wanted to convey an air of wistful intelligence and safety.

In her booth, the woman sipped her drink and waited for a message that would never come. Remick wished she would take her hat off so that he could admire her hair again, but it was clearly not that sort of a day. He contented himself with stealing glimpses of her face, each one imprinted onto his mind like a snapshot. Even in sadness her face was exquisite. Her mouth, devoid of make-up and turned down at the corners with misery, had full lips over which Remick longed to run his index finger. Her eyes glistened, not with the mischief that he had seen before, but with tears. Remick could bear her sadness no longer; closing his book, he picked up his coffee and went over to her booth.

"Excuse me. Would you mind if I join you?"

She shrugged and turned away, staring at the rivulets of condensation trickling down the window.

"It's a horrible day," Remick observed, doing the *let's talk about the weather* thing everyone seemed to do.

"Nice for ducks," the woman replied, not looking at him.

"I think the ducks are getting a bit fed up now." Remick took a sip of his latte, waiting for a response. When none came, he tried again. "They do a great latte here, I'll say that."

"I don't drink coffee," she said. "Green tea."

Remick sighed. This was not going to be quite as easy as he'd thought. He opened his book at another random location and began to read, watching the woman in his peripheral vision. He turned several pages before she paid him any heed.

"You read Proust?" she asked.

"Now and again, when the mood strikes me."

"In French?"

"That's how he wrote it. It seems rude not to."

"I tried reading it once." She shrugged dismissively. "I couldn't get into it. Maybe it's because I read it in English."

Remick put the book down. "It's a bit too sad for today anyway. It's miserable enough out there." He studied the watch he always wore on his wrist, even though it never told the correct time. "Is it that time already? I'm sorry, I've got to go. Lovely meeting you."

Then, in a move that had been carefully planned, he stood up and hurried out of the coffee shop without waiting for a reply, leaving the book on the table. Protruding from the pages was a business card—one of a box of a hundred Remick had ordered from a local printers—on which was the fictional name 'R. Thompson' and the number of a mobile phone he had bought especially for this purpose. He wondered if she would find the card and ring the number. He very much hoped that she would.

5.

THE PHONE RANG an hour and seventeen minutes later. Remick was sitting in another coffee shop two streets away from where he had left her. He was not keen on this coffee shop; the latte was distinctly substandard. Whereas the latte in the other place was thick and smooth with the partly sweet, partly bitter tang of good Ethiopian coffee, the one he was drinking at the moment was just warm and wet with hardly any flavour at all.

He watched, fascinated, as the display on the phone lit up and a merry electronic tune announced that a call was coming in. In all his time in this world, Remick had never owned one of the devices that held everyone captive, and he let it ring so long that it stopped. Remick was uncharacteristically unsure what to do next, but then a message popped up on the screen telling him that he had *one new voicemail*.

Remick had never had a voicemail before and was very intrigued by this new word, a word which when you broke it down actually made no sense. You either used your voice, or you used the mail, but not both. He picked the phone up and studied it and after a few moments of fumbling, found out how to access the recorded message. It thrilled him rather more than he had expected to hear a familiar voice emanating from the phone.

"Er...hello?" the voice said uncertainly. "I don't know if I've got the right number. Is this Mr. Thompson? Well, no, I know it's Mr. Thompson because that's the name on the card. If you're the man I just spoke to in the coffee shop, you left your book behind. Call me back if you want and I'll get the book to you." There was a pause, while she tried to decide what to say next. "If it's not you, I'm sorry to bother you. Anyway, my name is Angie and my number is…" She recited a number, which Remick did not need to write down. He had an exceptional memory. He put the phone down on the table and smiled. *Angie.*

Remick resisted the urge to call her back. He resisted it for exactly fourteen minutes, during which he wondered if she might call again. Then he decided to save her the cost of another call and, feeling strangely nervous, dialled the number he had memorised. She answered on the third ring.

"Hello?"

"Oh, yes, hello. Is this…er…Angie?"

"Yes it is. Who…? Oh. Thank you for calling back."

"Not at all. Thank *you* for taking the trouble to ring me. You found my book, I believe."

"Yes, I did. You left it on the table. By the time I realised, you'd gone. I wasn't sure if the card was yours."

"I like to use it as a bookmark. I hate people turning the corners of pages."

"Oh God, so do I! It ruins a book. I always use a bookmark."

"I'm very pleased to hear it. I'm also a bit forgetful, so it's useful for people to be able to contact me when I leave books in coffee shops."

He heard her laugh on the other end of the line and decided that he loved her laugh. It was a throaty, genuine laugh and he wanted to hear it more.

"So how can I get your book back to you?" she asked.

"Well I'm often in the coffee shop around that time. Maybe if you're passing sometime…?"

"I could drop it in tomorrow," she suggested.

"That would be…oh no, wait. I'm busy tomorrow. Would Thursday be any good to you?"

"Thursday's fine. About one? I'm on my lunch then."

"Perfect. Thank you so much. It's only a cheap paperback, but it does have sentimental value. I'll buy you a green tea for your trouble."

"Deal. Oh, look, I have to go. I've got a customer. I'll see you on Thursday, Mr. Thompson."

"You can call me Remick."

"Remy? Okay, Remy. See you Thursday."

He did not see fit to correct her. She called him Remy, so Remy he would be. It was just one lie in a call full of them. He had never left a book in a coffee shop before, the book had no sentimental value—although it might just acquire some now—and he was not particularly busy tomorrow. He did not want to appear too keen and risk unsettling her. In any case, time meant little to him. He could make it Thursday right now if he wished. So he did.

6.

Remick was so used to living his life in a non-linear way that he felt sorry for anyone who did not. How frustrating it must be for them to have to wait for things. In seconds, he had stepped out of Tuesday into Thursday and was walking the short distance from one coffee shop to another. He only hoped that the woman—Angie—did not judge him harshly for not changing his clothes. He knew these things could sometimes be important.

Thursday was raining again. Judging by the pools of water which had accumulated in the gutters and spread across parts of the road as the drains were unable to cope, Wednesday had seen it fair share of rainfall too. Remick had to jump over one large puddle but managed to do it without getting his boots wet. Not that it mattered; these boots had seen far worse than a bit of water. He had chosen to arrive in Thursday at six minutes past one. He could, if he wanted, be there at precisely one to the second, but not everybody had the same regard for time he did, and she had said 'about one', after all.

He shook some of the rainwater off his coat sleeves as he stepped into the coffee shop, where Angie was sitting in the same booth as last time. She smiled when she saw him and did a kind of half-wave. He returned it and, noticing she did not yet have a drink, gestured to the counter. She nodded and smiled again. It was a magnificent smile.

Remick bought a latte and a green tea, and carried them carefully over to the booth. He did not yet know whether she felt as strongly as he did about drink slopped into the saucer, nor did he want to find out. He placed the cups on the table and sat down.

"Hi," she said, still with a smile that warmed Remick more than any latte could. "You came."

"Well, of course I did. You've got my book."

Confusion momentarily crossed her face, but Remick grinned to show he was joking, and she relaxed.

"And I owe you a green tea," he added. "I don't know if you want anything to eat…"

"No, I'm fine, thanks. I had a sandwich back at the shop."

Remick allowed himself a moment to look at her. Today, she was dressed not in grey, but in the red coat she had been wearing when he first saw her, complemented by a russet-coloured scarf decorated with an intricate and delicate design in black. No hat, her ebony hair hung loose.

He must have let his gaze linger for too long, because she frowned and asked, "What?"

"I…er… I like your scarf," he replied, cursing himself inwardly.

"Do you? Yes, so do I. I got it from the market. There's a stall that sells hundreds of them, but this one just caught my eye." She took a sip of her tea, then reached into a tan leather bag at her side. "Your book," she said, putting it on the table and pushing it towards him.

"Thank you, but you didn't have to go to this trouble."

"It's no trouble. Really. So…Remy. Is that French? It's just with the Proust and everything…"

"Yes, it is," he confirmed, even though he had not really thought about it until now. "A couple of generations back. My…er…grandfather. Came over after the war."

"Do you go there much? France, I mean."

"Funnily enough, I've never been there." He'd been just about everywhere. "I will one day. And Angie. Is that short for…?"

"Evangeline." She laughed. "Yes, I know. Sounds like I've come from the Bayou." She said this with a Southern American accent which did something to Remick that he liked. "My grandparents were from Jamaica, though." She switched her accent to Jamaican. "But I've never been there either."

"How do you do that?" Remick asked. "The accents. They're perfect."

"You think?" She beamed. "I should be an actress. Good ear, I guess. But when my grandma talks like that alllll the time…"

"So, what do you do? You said something about a shop?"

"I manage a concession in Doyle's. You know, the department store on Parker Street? I've got the china concession. Yes, I know. It's a job. It's not forever. What about you? What do you do? Your card didn't really say."

Remick was suddenly aware that he should have prepared a bit better for this. He was not used to human contact and certainly not used to conversation. He said the first thing that came into his head. "I repair clocks. And watches."

"Really?" Her eyes went wide. "Wow. I'd never have said that. I thought you were a musician or something. Wow. That's amazing."

"Not really." He feigned modesty. "My father taught me."

"Look, this is going to sound really cheeky…" She pushed her coat sleeve up and unbuckled a watch from her wrist. "Could you take a look at this for me? It's always slow. I guess that's why I'm always late. It's okay, say no if you want." She passed the watch over to him.

"Of course I will," he agreed without the slightest idea how he was going to do it. He examined the watch, trying to look like an expert. It was quite a plain piece: a steel case and a worn black leather strap. The black Roman numerals on the dial were slightly faded with age, and Remick could see at a glance that the second hand was running fractionally slower than it should. It was four minutes and twenty-seven seconds slow.

"It's a lovely watch," he said.

"My grandma gave it to me for my twenty-first," Angie explained. "My grandpa gave it to her. It means a lot."

Remick ran his fingers over the watch, and in his mind's eye, he saw a young man, uncomfortable in the first new suit he had ever owned, handing over money in a shop in exchange for this watch, brand-new and gleaming in a black velvet-lined gift box. Remick felt the pride and love with which this watch had been purchased and it tugged at his heart.

"It was the first thing he bought her," he said, barely aware he was speaking.

Angie gasped, astounded. "Yes, it was! He bought it with his first wages. How did you know?"

"Just a guess," Remick answered. "Yes, of course I'll fix it for you. I'd be honoured. I'll call you when it's ready."

"I'll pay," Angie offered. "Doesn't matter what it costs. I'd love it to be working properly."

"Don't be silly. I'll do it as a gift. No charge."

"No, that's not right," she protested. "You hardly know me. And you've got to make a living."

"All right," Remick conceded. "The price is one latte when I bring your watch back."

"You're mad!" She laughed. "But okay. One latte."

Yes, Remick thought. Yes, he must be mad for offering to fix the watch without any idea how to accomplish it. But it was a very pleasant madness and one he was prepared to embrace.

She left shortly afterwards, apologising for having to get back to work, but she thanked him once again and touched him on his arm as she departed.

Remick stayed the coffee shop for a long time after that, staring at the second hand of the watch as it ticked around, feeling that touch on his arm and for once unsure about what to do next.

7.

REMICK SPENT SOME time in the room he used as lodgings, staring at the watch and wondering what to do. He could simply visit the time and place where it had been bought and buy another one that was the same. Seeing as he knew the exact time and place, nothing would have been easier. However, there were problems with this plan, the first and most obvious being that the shop might only have had one watch like it, and Remick couldn't just buy one that was similar. Even if he found the same brand and model, what if it had a serial number or something and Angie recognised the one she had now was different? He did not yet know enough about her to be able to tell how closely she had studied the watch.

But the real problem was that this—even if it worked—was an untidy solution. Of course, there would be other worlds on which he could have bought the self-same watch before Angie's grandfather did, but that would mean depriving the Angies of those worlds of the pleasure of receiving and owning the watch. In any case, Remick had promised to repair the watch, not replace it with a similar one. If he were to have any kind of relationship with Angie, it could not start with a broken promise. It would have to be done the hard way.

So Remick took himself to a different time and place and, after some searching, located an elderly watchmaker for whom the work was getting too much. For a financial consideration, which Remick was only too happy to provide, the watchmaker agreed to take him under his wing and train him.

Remick spent what amounted to several years with the watchmaker, working and training and learning and listening to the old man's stories. Only then was he confident enough to take the back off Angie's watch and look inside. He was nervous about stripping the watch down and cleaning and oiling the component parts, and the first time he did it, he was almost happy. The watch was now only losing a small amount of time, but it was still losing, and Remick wanted it to be perfect, so he did it again.

This time, the watch was as near completely accurate as any device made by man could be, and by the time he had polished the case and carefully cleaned the surface of the dial, he was satisfied that the watch had been restored to a very good state, one that belied its age. He was reluctant, in a way, to take his leave of the old watchmaker but was pleased that he had been able to provide him with some companionship in the last years of his life.

Remick took the watch and returned to Angie's world and time but still waited for several days, checking and rechecking the timekeeping of the watch before he turned on his mobile phone and called her to tell her it was ready. Three years had passed for Remick. A week had passed for her.

8.

THEY MET IN the coffee shop once again. Remick had wondered whether the time was right yet to try meeting somewhere else, but decided that, for now, the coffee shop was safe and familiar. The day was another wet one, just as four out of the seven days since they last met had been. There was talk that it could turn out to be one of the wettest spells on record. Rural areas were beset by flooding as rivers swelled and overflowed their banks. Here in the city, it was just very wet.

When Remick arrived at the coffee shop, Angie was already there, sitting expectantly in the corner booth with drinks on the table.

"I bought you a latte," she said as Remick wiped the rain from his face with a napkin. "Is that okay? If you'd rather have something else..."

Remick found the concern in Angie's lovely face touching and surprising. She wanted to please him; it was not something he experienced often.

"No, no, that's perfect," he replied, sitting down. He sampled the coffee and made exaggerated *mmm* noises of approval. "But you didn't have to."

"Of course I did. You've fixed my watch for me. A deal's a deal. You *have* fixed it, haven't you?" Her face shone with such a childlike eagerness that Remick could wait no longer. He reached into his inside pocket and with a flourish produced the watch. She took it from him and compared the time with the time displayed on her phone.

"It's spot on! Pretty much to the second! That's wonderful. And you've cleaned the dial and everything. I've never seen it look like this. Thank you, Remy. Thank you so much."

"It's my pleasure," Remick replied and meant it. "It's a good watch. It deserves to be looked after. May I?"

He reached over and, taking the watch from her, fastened it securely on her wrist. She held her hand away from her to admire how it looked.

"Are you sure I don't owe you anything? I feel bad about not paying. All the time you've put in…"

If only you knew, Remick thought, but instead said, "It didn't take that long, really. It's a gift, Angie. A gift to brighten up a miserable day."

"It's done that, all right," Angie told him. "Thank you. Nobody has ever done anything like this for me."

"What, nobody? I can't believe that. Surely you have a boyfriend or someone to do nice things for you?"

"I did have…" Angie cloud passed over her face. "He wasn't really that much of a boyfriend, but he was…*someone*, I suppose. And no, he didn't do many nice things for me."

"What happened?" Remick asked, putting on an expression of concern.

"I don't know. He just stopped calling me. He didn't call me that often, anyway—only when he was bored or lonely and wanted to see me. But he just stopped completely, and when I tried calling him…it was like he had just vanished. I even went to his office, and the people in the other offices said he'd just up and left."

"That seems like a strange thing to do. You must have been very worried."

"I thought about telling the police or someone, but he's a grown man. What can they do? I knew his business was in trouble. While I was with him, he kept getting calls from people he owed money to. He tried not to let me hear, but I did. I think he just ran away from it all. And from me."

Remick risked reaching across the table to take her hand. She let him, and he marvelled at how warm and smooth her hand was in his.

"Now, you listen to me," he said. "He obviously wasn't worth it. If he could just walk away from you, he can't have cared enough about you. The man was a fool to leave you. I know I couldn't have done it."

Angie squeezed his hand and smiled. Even though the smile was tempered with regret, there was warmth in it.

"That's sweet," she said. "I thought I'd done something for a bit, but now I just think sod it. It's his loss."

"It is indeed," Remick agreed. "Very much so."

"Thank you. I suppose I needed to hear that. Look, Remy, would you like to have dinner with me one night?" Remick must have looked shocked, because Angie let go of his hand. "Sorry! I just blurted that out. I'm such an idiot. You could be married or anything for all I know. I'm sorry, I just say things sometimes without thinking!"

"Angie…" Remick took her hand again. "Angie. It's okay. I'm not married. Or anything. I would love to have dinner with you. I was just a bit surprised that someone like you would even think about it."

"Someone like me?" Angie laughed. "I'm not all that, Remy. Not when you get to know me. You haven't seen me at my worst."

"I'd like to," Remick said and in all his years had never meant anything more. "I'd like to get to know you at your worst and your best. But I definitely think we should start with dinner."

And that settled it. They arranged to meet two nights later at a restaurant they both knew. Then they talked of other insignificant things until it was time for Angie to return to work. Remick walked with her through the rain, which no longer touched him, and left her outside the store. She waved briefly as she went through the revolving door and then was gone. Remick felt her absence immediately and stood outside for a long time.

9.

REMICK STOOD IN front of the mirror in the room he used and studied his reflection. He was not accustomed to looking in mirrors as a general rule. He saw no purpose in vanity and seldom did anything without a purpose. But he was aware that the rest of the race among whom he walked were often very concerned about the way they looked and, although Angie had not seemed overly bothered by his appearance so far, he wanted to make a good impression. This seemed to be very much a time of firsts. So, to that end, he studied himself in the mirror and tried to see himself through her eyes.

It was not especially easy; he was still only learning bit by bit what her eyes saw. The look he currently wore was not, he supposed, a bad one by the standards of this time and on this world. That was partly why he had chosen it. He did not carry excessive weight, he had reasonably good bone structure, and all his features were more or less where they were intended to be. If one looked closely at his eyes, one might imagine they were they eyes of someone who had seen a great deal in their time, and he would have to be careful to curb their occasional tendency to flare up with crimson fire, but otherwise he was fairly confident that he was relatively pleasing to look at.

His beard could perhaps do with a trim, and he did wonder about whether he should find something with which to tie his hair back, but then, he decided, that was not really him and he wanted Angie to know *him*, or at least, as much of him as he could reveal without making her run away screaming. Instead, he found a comb in one of his pockets—without the slightest idea how it had got there—and ran it with some difficulty through his hair.

The only other change he made was to put on a new dark-blue shirt he had procured. Then he was ready to arrive at the restaurant at seven: the time they had arranged. He had booked the table for seven-thirty, so they would have time for a drink beforehand. There had been no reservations available for that time initially, so Remick had had to go back a few days and find a day before anyone else had booked. It took a few tries, but he managed it eventually. It had not occurred to him that the restaurant might be so popular.

He was waiting outside at three minutes to seven. They might have agreed on seven, but Remick knew enough to understand that when ordinary people specified a time, there was usually a significant margin for error. As a result, when seven o'clock arrived and Angie had not, Remick was not really surprised. It did not even matter that there had been no let up in the rain because the restaurant had an awning outside, so he could wait without getting his new shirt wet.

When first five past and then ten past came with no sign of Angie, he was initially irritated, then increasingly worried that she might not be coming. Maybe she had changed her mind. Remick had not been able to read her well enough to know if this was the sort of thing she might do. It came as a considerable relief, then, when at thirteen minutes past seven he saw her hurrying around the corner.

"Sorry," she said as she approached. "Half the buses seemed to have been cancelled, and then the one I did get took forever. I don't know if it's the weather or what." She paused and then startled him by kissing him quickly on the cheek. "Hello. Sorry. Have you been waiting long?"

"No," he lied. "I've just got here myself."

"And there's me with a newly fixed watch and everything. Come on, then, let's go in before they give our table to someone else. We should still be able to grab a drink. Am I talking too much? I do that sometimes when I'm nervous. I don't know why I'm nervous. *Am* I talking too much?"

"No, you're not," Remick reassured her, holding open the restaurant door. "I like to hear you talk. And there's nothing to be nervous about. It's just dinner."

The restaurant was warm inside, and the air was fragrant with cooking. A dinner-suited waiter carefully checked their reservation, trying very hard to disguise his contempt for Remick's appearance with a veneer of perfect manners. He offered to take Angie's coat, which she declined, but he stopped short of wanting to handle Remick's and then showed them to their table. By the time they sat down, it was obvious that Angie was struggling to contain her amusement. The waiter oozed off to get some menus, and as soon as he had gone, Angie burst out laughing.

"Oh my god! What a knob!" she said as she shrugged off her coat. "I'm sorry, but he is." Then she stopped, catching the serious expression on Remick's face. "I haven't offended you, have I? I just say things sometimes."

"Of course not," Remick said with a grin. "You're right. He *is* a knob. No, I was just about to say how beautiful you look."

"Shut up! Do I?"

Remick thought it was possible he had never seen anyone more beautiful. She was wearing a simple black dress with a high neckline, and her only jewellery was a pair of small pearl stud earrings. Her hair was loosely plaited and hung over one shoulder and was tied at the end with a black ribbon. Remick was no expert on make-up, but she appeared to be wearing hardly any at all. He was aware he was staring but found he was unable to look away.

"Yes," he said. "You do."

"Well, thank you, Remy," she replied, smiled, then changed the subject. "The watch is keeping great time, by the way. Did I say that?"

"You did, but it's still good to hear."

They were interrupted by a discreet cough from the waiter, who handed them leather-bound menus and then withdrew.

"Wow, look at this!" Angie exclaimed, opening her menu. "Real leather and everything. Have you eaten here before?"

"Not recently, no. It's supposed to be very good."

"Look at the prices! Remy, it's really expensive."

"It's fine. Don't worry, really."

Angie raised an eyebrow. "You must have repaired a lot of watches recently. And charged for them. You don't get to eat here if you do them all for nothing like you did with mine."

Remick had to think fast. He never really gave money much consideration, as he had many ways of acquiring it. He had never met anyone who'd questioned it.

"I don't rely on the watch repairs," was the best he could come up with. "That's more a sort of hobby. I've got—shall we say— other sources of income."

"Say no more," Angie said. "I won't ask. As long as you're sure. I was going to suggest going halves."

"It's fine, really. Have whatever you want."

Angie frowned briefly, then tilted her head in a *whatever you say* gesture. "I just hope it's worth it. I'd hate to see you paying all that for a smear of sauce and a piece of lettuce on a slate."

When the waiter returned with his pad, Remick waited until Angie ordered and then ordered the same and passed it off as a remarkable coincidence. In truth, he didn't actually need food, so it meant little to him, but he thought that at least pretending to have the same tastes as Angie would give them some common ground. As long as it was nothing too rich in iron, it would not give him any problems. He ordered a bottle of what looked like a good wine and the waiter disappeared off through a set of double doors at the back of the restaurant.

While they waited for their food, Remick and Angie made small talk, something he had never found easy before. His mind was usually on higher things, but they were not things he could chat about now, if ever. Instead, he let Angie tell him all about her day at work and some of the amusing or even irritating customers she had served, and he surprised himself by finding her conversation interesting and entertaining. It helped that she told the stories so well, making full use of the talent for mimicry he had seen in her before, but more than that, he just felt as though he could listen to her forever. He decided then and there that was exactly what he would like to do.

The food arrived, and, for Angie's sake, he was relieved that it was considerably more substantial than the smear and lettuce she had described. Angie ate with obvious enjoyment, and Remick found pleasure in her pleasure. He ate his food too. Even though it tasted of nothing to him, he found himself agreeing with her enthusiastic remarks about the flavouring of the sauce and the expert cooking of the lamb. He enjoyed the wine rather more but took care to sip it and make it last.

All too soon, they had finished their meal, even though Remick did his best to prolong it by insisting first on desserts and then on coffee.

As she drank her coffee, Angie leaned back in her chair and sighed happily. "That was gorgeous," she said. "I'll have to fast for days, but it was worth it. I feel absolutely stuffed. Thank you, Remy."

"My pleasure. We must do this again."

"I'd love to. But maybe not somewhere quite as expensive as this. Do you know what I'd like? I'd really like to go for a picnic. Somewhere by a river or something. Looks like I'll have to wait for a bit, though. I don't think we're going to see summer anytime soon."

"Funny you should say that, but I've heard next weekend is going to be perfect for picnics," Remick told her impulsively.

"That's not the forecast I heard."

"They always get it wrong. No, trust me, Saturday is going to be perfect. What do you think? Shall we?"

"I can't Remy. I'm in work on Saturday."

"Take the day off."

"I can't just do that. It isn't fair."

"When was the last day you took off?"

"Ages ago, but… No, you're right. Helen can cope for one day without me. She's done it before."

"That's settled, then."

"Well, if you're sure…"

"I am."

"And as long as you're not getting fed up with me…"

"That won't happen either. I promise."

"Well, okay, then. But if we get drenched, it's all your fault."

They agreed a time that Remick fully expected Angie would not keep to, and he paid the bill, leaving the waiter a reasonably generous tip. Outside, it was still raining, and Angie put up an umbrella she had been concealing in her bag. So that Remick could share the umbrella, she linked her arm through his as they walked. When they reached her bus stop, she turned to face him, standing so close he could smell the delicate perfume she was wearing.

"Thank you for a lovely evening, Remy. I won't invite you back, if you don't mind. Not this time. I'm just a bit tired."

Then she leaned in close and kissed him briefly and softly on the mouth.

"Goodnight, Remy," she said, as her bus arrived. She climbed aboard, leaving Remick looking at the rain-soaked street and wondering just how he was going to make a summer's day out of winter.

10.

WHENEVER HE ENCOUNTERED a problem which appeared insoluble, Remick was inclined to take himself off to the place where he found it easiest to think. He went back to the beginning, when the worlds were new, a time when life had not begun and problems were yet to occur. The landscape was harsh and uninviting, but Remick was able to sit on a rock he had sculpted into the rough shape of a seat and gaze out onto an arena filled with almost infinite possibilities. The fact that he knew how many of those possibilities would develop did not stop him from contemplating the wonder of it all and allowed him to think with a clarity he could not find elsewhere.

In theory, the answer to his current problem seemed obvious. He could either wait for a summer's day to occur or take Angie to a summer's day that had already existed. Both options had their drawbacks; the first was out of the question because Remick just did not want to wait. If he had been able to see further along Angie's timeline, he could have checked whether her feelings remained the same or even became stronger, but as her future was a blank to him, he was not prepared to take the risk.

The second option was better, but he was not yet prepared to reveal his true nature to Angie and was not sure he ever would. She believed him to be human, and he thought, quite correctly, it might be a bit too early in their relationship to demonstrate to her that he was not. If he could not take her to another time—nor wait for that time to happen—he would have to bring another time to her.

That was where the problems really arose. Remick could not just take a day of time from one place and put it somewhere else because it would be noticed. Somewhere down the line, it would be apparent that the order of things had been disturbed, and even if Remick were able to put the day back, it would have been changed by his and Angie's presence. The changes might only be small but would inevitably lead to bigger ones. Remick had made enough mistakes in his many years of existence to know that time had to be handled carefully, or there could be dire consequences. Even if he felt inclined to try, there were rules preventing him from doing so and the rules were made by forces whose power he dared not think about.

Remick was left with just one option: he would have to build a summer's day, minute by minute, with time stolen from as many other days as he could find and hope no-one noticed.

That beautiful, warm day when a grey cloud suddenly crosses the sun and you think it might rain, but then the cloud is gone and the day is perfect again? That was Remick stealing a couple of minutes and replacing it with a couple of minutes from a day that was not so fine. That time when you are sitting outside in the sun and an unexpected cool breeze raises goosebumps on your skin? That was Remick too.

Little by little, piece by piece, Remick dismantled Saturday and replaced it with the most glorious Saturday he could build. It was long, painstaking and exhausting work, taking moments out of time and then moving them back into a different place. It was a colossal juggling act, the like of which Remick had seldom attempted before, but when he had finished, there was a perfect Saturday just waiting for Angie, and the best part of all? It was sealed in a capsule of its own time so that she could enjoy it and explore it over and over for as long as her heart desired. She would never have to put up with the rain again.

There was only one thing left to do, and it was the easy part. Remick would buy the best ingredients he could find to make the most delicious, sumptuous picnic Angie had ever seen.

11.

On Saturday morning, while Angie was waking up early to find the rain had ceased and sunlight was streaming through her window, and while Remick tried to remember how to drive the car he had just acquired, a man named Derek Benson was arriving at the newsagent's shop he owned to start sorting through the morning's newspapers. He was quite surprised to find an unexpected addition to his delivery this particular Saturday. There was a body lying outside his shop.

He was only quite surprised, rather than very surprised, because this was a Saturday, after all, and sometimes strange things went on in this neighbourhood on Friday nights. He often had to step over uneaten takeaway meals, half-empty pint glasses, vomit, and, on one notable occasion, various items of ladies' underclothing on the pavement outside his shop. Up until now, however, he had never before found a body.

It appeared to be that of a man in maybe his early thirties. It was hard to tell because he was partially concealed by the bales of plastic-wrapped newspapers. Reaching for his phone, Derek approached cautiously and stopped. He was sure he'd seen the man's leg twitch, but he still kept his finger poised to dial the emergency services. The man might not be dead, but he'd probably need an ambulance, or Derek might need the police. He continued to approach with caution.

As he drew near, the man suddenly sat bolt upright, startling Derek so much that he dropped his phone—something he would later discover caused a crack in the screen that would cost nearly half a day's takings to fix.

"Are you okay, mate?" Derek asked. "Are you hurt?"

The man just stared, looking around, disorientated, which Derek put down to drink or drugs or more likely both. He was even more convinced of this when the man said, "I'm back!"

"Yes you are," Derek humoured him. "You're okay now. Just take it easy?"

"Take it easy?" Brian Norris echoed. "Take it easy? He's got to be stopped, don't you see? He's the Devil! He's got to be stopped!"

Then he slumped back against the bales of newspapers, and Derek decided it was time to call an ambulance. The papers were going to be slightly delayed today.

12.

THERE WAS A moment, just as Remick halted the car outside Angie's building, when he had a horrible feeling he had forgotten something. Warm sunlight streamed through the car windscreen, and the half wound-down window was letting in just the right amount of breeze to make the temperature bearable. There was hardly a cloud in the sky, and the rain seemed a very long way away.

All around, people were starting their day and leaving their houses, surprised by the weather. Everyone had been expecting more rain, and Remick saw several people dash back into their houses to leave coats behind. One or two still carried umbrellas, though. It was as well to be safe.

The Saturday Remick had created was perfect, but there was something wrong, something he had missed. As the door opened and Angie emerged, Remick sensed it. The man, Norris. He was somewhere here. Somehow, as Remick had taken his stolen moments out of time and brought them back into their new place, Norris had come back with one of them. Remick cursed himself briefly, but he had dealt with Norris before and could do so again. Then he saw Angie and every other thought went out of his head.

He saw her before she saw him, and he had the opportunity to observe her delight as she shut the door behind her and stood on the step, looking up to the sky and basking in the sun's rays as they warmed her face. She was wearing a pale-blue dress decorated with a subtle floral print, and her hair was tied casually back with a silk scarf in a matching colour. A brown suede bag was slung over her shoulder. The dress left her arms bare, and Remick could almost feel her pleasure as she felt the sun on her skin. He smiled with quiet amusement to see that, just like everyone else who did not quite trust the sudden good weather, she had a coat over her arm. Then she spotted him, and her smile almost eclipsed the sun. She ran over to the car and threw open the passenger door.

"You did it! Look at the weather! It's a beautiful day! How did you know? This wasn't forecast!"

"Lucky guess," Remick replied. "Jump in. I know the perfect place for a picnic."

Angie climbed in and tossed her coat onto the back seat. "I don't think I'll be needing that."

"I'm absolutely sure you won't. It's going to be like this all day."

"And look at you! You've even left your coat behind. I've never seen you without it. You look...different. In a good way."

She stopped talking and leaned over to kiss him on the cheek. As she did so, he inhaled her perfume, a tang of citrus.

"Thank you for this," she said. "I think it's going to be just what I need. Come on! Let's go!"

Remick allowed himself to be swept away by her enthusiasm and started the car.

"Where are we going?" she asked. "Or is it a surprise?"

"Not really. I thought we might go to the beach."

"Really? I haven't had a picnic on the beach for... God, *years*! Not since I was a kid. What a brilliant idea. Pity I haven't got a bucket and spade."

Remick drove out of the city and past the docks with their container ships and scrap metal yards. In the sunlight, the grey streets were transformed and the ships were magnificent. Angie foraged in her bag and pulled out a pair of sunglasses and put them on.

"I almost couldn't find these, it's been that long."

As they drove, Angie kept up an excited monologue, mostly about the weather and how jealous anyone would be who was in work on a day like this. She said she felt a bit bad for her assistant, Helen, who would be stuck in the shop while Angie swanned off on picnics, but, hey, Helen had phoned in with hangovers before now, so she'd have to get on with it just this once. Remick listened, added the occasional reply, but mainly concentrated on driving. This was not the day to crash a car.

After half an hour or so, they had driven through deprived, shuttered suburbs and more affluent, tree-lined ones and parked the car in a designated—and expensive—car park, which, even at this time of the day, was filling up as everyone had the same idea.

"Everywhere's dried up really quickly," Angie observed as they got out of the car. "You'd think it would be soaking after all the rain we've had."

"Must be the sand," Remick replied, guessing at something that might sound plausible. "It'll just absorb the water."

"I hope the beach is dry. I don't want to sit on damp sand."

Remick opened the boot of the car and took out a picnic basket and a folded plaid blanket.

"Well, just in case…"

"You've thought of everything, haven't you?"

"I hope so," Remick said. "I've tried."

As they walked from the car to the beach, he carried the picnic basket in one hand and the blanket under his arm, leaving the hand nearest Angie free. As he had hoped, she slipped her hand into his, throwing him a glance as if to say *you don't mind, do you?* He smiled reassurance back but said nothing, fearing that if he did, it would break the spell and she might pull away. Her hand felt warm and comfortable in his and he did not want to let go, but when they reached the ideal spot on the beach, a good flat patch of clean sand slightly sheltered by dunes, he had to let go to spread the blanket out. They sat down side by side, and this time, when their fingers touched and intertwined, there was no need to let go.

They sat in silence for a while, watching dogs tear around the beach, enjoying a freedom they had not had for months.

"So tell me about yourself," Angie said. "I know you're a part-time watchmaker, a pretty damn good weather forecaster and brilliant at organising picnics, but other than that... Who are you, Remy? I feel like I've known you ages yet hardly know you at all."

"I'm no-one special," Remick replied. "I've been around a bit, done some things. Nothing really interesting."

"You're too modest. I think you're a very nice man, that's what I think. Can I guess? I think...I think your parents are rich, but maybe they've made their money in something you don't like? You've rebelled by growing your hair and pretending to be someone ordinary. Am I close?"

"Close enough."

"But you're not ordinary, are you? There's something extraordinary about you. I don't know what it is, but I'll find out."

"No, really, I'm not that exciting. I'd rather talk about you. Tell me all about Evangeline."

"Not much to tell there, either," Angie said, looking out to sea. "All very typical. Parents came here looking for a better life for themselves and for me and worked damn hard to get it. Sent me off to school and told me to study and be the best I could be. And I tried. I really tried. But, I don't know, the teachers seemed to be more interested in the kids who were, well, whiter than me, and I sort of stopped trying. I left school as soon as I could—which broke my mum's heart, I can tell you—and tried to get a job. My dad had a heart attack when I was sixteen and couldn't work, so someone had to bring some money in. My mum was working all the hours she could, but it wasn't enough. Then my dad died, and it just got harder."

A solitary tear trickled down Angie's cheek. Remick reached out and brushed it away with one finger. She rewarded him with a weak smile.

"I shouldn't be getting into all the sad stuff. This is supposed to be a lovely, happy day out."

"I'm with you and getting to know you. It *is* a happy day."

"That's sweet of you. Looks like I was right about you being a nice man."

"Tell me more. You were looking for a job…?"

"Same story. Plenty of jobs out there if your face fits—or rather if the *colour* of your face fits. Or if you want to work in a burger place. I really, really didn't want to work in a burger place."

"I don't understand this thing about skin colour," Remick said. "I don't see why it bothers people. Take the skin off and everyone looks the same."

"You are definitely a rare one," Angie replied. "Luckily, the owners of Doyle's think like that too. They gave me a job in the underwear department of all places and I took it. That means I have really nice underwear, by the way. Just saying."

This flirtatious candour caught Remick by surprise and he found he did not have a good answer. Instead, he said, "But you're not on—er—*that* department now."

"No. I did two years on it, though, which I didn't expect. Then the assistant manager on the china department left, and I was asked, actually asked, to go for the job. I got it, too, and I really didn't expect that. Then the manager retired last year, and they didn't even advertise the job. They just gave it to me. They've been so good to me there, Remy, and I love it. I love being around beautiful things."

"You should be surrounded by beauty," Remick told her. "It suits you."

"Annnyway!" Angie laughed, all tears forgotten. "Enough about me. All the time we've been talking, I've been thinking about one thing. What's in that hamper you brought? Come on, Remy, get it open!"

Remick opened the hamper, and it did not disappoint. It was filled with freshly baked breads, cooked meats and the finest cheeses he had been able to get. Angie ate ravenously, savouring every mouthful and remarking on everything she sampled. Remick ate too and found that Angie's appetite and clear enjoyment of the food made it taste better to him. Eventually, Angie stopped eating and sat back on the blanket.

"That was so good," she said. "Thank you. I'd better stop now or I'll be the size of a house."

"That isn't possible," Remick answered. "You're perfect as you are."

Angie wiped some crumbs from her lips with the back of her hand, and then snaked an arm around Remick's shoulders, drawing him close. When she leaned in and kissed him, it nearly took his breath away. Then she pulled him down onto the blanket, and time stopped altogether.

13.

I WISH THIS DAY could go on forever," Angie said, lying with her head on Remick's chest. They were in her bed and had just made love for the second time. The first time had been rushed and urgent, starting the instant they had crossed the threshold of her flat. The second time had been slower, more tender and longer-lasting. Now Angie drowsed in Remick's arms.

"It will be back tomorrow," Remick replied, stroking her hair. "Tomorrow's Sunday."

But it wasn't. Tomorrow was Saturday again.

14.

O N THE SECOND Saturday, Remick loaded the hamper in the car and drove to Angie's building. She answered the door to him with a faintly disappointed look on her face. She had, she explained, hoped he would be there when she woke up, but he had gone with no note, no message, nothing. Remick showed her the picnic hamper in the car and told her to be ready to leave in ten minutes. Understanding that he had only left her to go and prepare today's treat, Angie had brightened immediately and scampered back upstairs to her flat.

Remick sat in the car and waited. Refilling the picnic hamper was not the only thing he had done since he had left Angie sleeping in her bed. He had also done some searching and located Brian Norris. He had been considerably reassured to discover that Norris was currently in hospital, having been found lying in the street, and was receiving psychiatric care because he was raving about being kidnapped by the Devil. This amused Remick greatly. There was no Devil, of course, but some of the upper hierarchy of his kind would not have been impressed that Remick had been mistaken for one of them. But while there was little chance that anyone would take Norris seriously, it was reasonably safe to leave him where he was.

On this second Saturday, Remick had decided to venture a little further and planned to take Angie to a charming little waterfall he knew of in Snowdonia. Somewhere remote suited him well, partly because he wanted to spend time with Angie alone and not share her with other people, but also because the further away from the city they were, the less chance there was of Angie spotting that this was not Sunday as she thought, but Saturday once again. He could only sustain the stolen Saturday for Angie, though; everyone else in the city would have to get their coats and umbrellas out again because more rain was due for their day. This was not something he felt like explaining to Angie just yet.

She emerged from her building, dressed in the same pale-blue floral print dress, and once she was in the car, they set off.

"You did it!" she said excitedly. "Look at the weather! It's a beautiful day! How did you know? This wasn't forecast!"

As soon as she said it, she stopped and frowned.

"Are you all right?" Remick asked. "Have you forgotten something?"

"No, it's the weirdest thing. I'm sure I've said that before."

"Déjà vu," Remick remarked. "Or it could just because you said it yesterday."

"Did I? Really? How did I forget that?"

"You've had other things on your mind."

"And elsewhere," Angie said with a giggle. "Speaking of which, thank you for last night.

Remick smiled a *you're welcome* and tried to drive on in silence for a while, but Angie had other ideas.

"It was okay, wasn't it? I mean, I'm a bit out of practice. Brian was more a vanilla sort of guy, if you know what I mean. I think I might have got a bit carried away."

"It was perfect, Angie, honestly." Remick tried to keep the irritation he felt at the mention of Norris's name out of his voice. "Don't worry. I'm not him."

"No," Angie agreed. "You're certainly not."

Remick took the compliment at face value but still did not welcome any comparison to Norris. Remick had lived a life and had abilities that a protoplasm like Norris could not even dream about, but he had spent time with Angie, slept with her, even meant something to her, and this gave rise to feelings in Remick he had not encountered before.

He imagined it could be called jealousy, and he had never had cause to be jealous of humans with their brief, petty lives. He should have erased the man from this timeline altogether while he had the chance. But then he looked over at Angie, who was watching the world shoot past through the half-open car window, a smile on her lips that he was not meant to see, a smile that was just for her, and he knew he was making her happy in a way Norris never had. For a while, that was sufficient.

They spoke very little throughout the journey, but Remick had now understood Angie intimately enough to know she talked a great deal when she was nervous. If she was content to be silent, then it meant she was relaxed and comfortable and he did not want to spoil that with unnecessary conversation. So he drove and she watched out of the window as the grey of town and motorway was replaced by the green of the countryside.

The road he had chosen wound around the base of the mountains of Snowdonia, through villages whose names had too many consonants, and began to climb upwards.

Angie let the window down the rest of the way and breathed in deeply, tasting the clean country air. "I know why dogs do this now."

"Dogs do lots of things. There aren't many of those I'd do, though."

Angie tried to bark but could not manage it for laughing. She was still laughing when Remick pulled the car into a lay-by and announced that they had arrived.

"Is this it?" Angie asked. "I mean, it's nice and everything…"

"I hope you've got sensible shoes on. There's a bit of a walk yet. This is as close as I can get the car."

Angie looked down at her feet. She was wearing a pair of shoes which looked to Remick to be constructed of several strips of blue leather and a lot of not much else. She shrugged.

"They'll have to do. If you'd told me in advance… You might end up having to carry me."

"I can't do that *and* carry the hamper. I'll just have to leave you and have the picnic on my own."

"Don't you dare!" She slapped him on the arm playfully, but hard enough. "Come on, then. Which way?"

Remick got the hamper and blanket out of the car and led Angie through a gate to a rough footpath. The path took them first across a rock-strewn field, then through a copse of trees with moss-lined trunks where the air was cool and moist. They paused there for a moment, and as they did, the sound of running water drifted through the trees.

"Is that a river?" Angie wanted to know.

"Better than that. Come and see."

They emerged from the copse onto the banks of a stream, which had carved its way through lichen covered rocks, but the sound of running water was coming from a waterfall which cascaded down the mountainside and fed the stream. Angie gazed at the waterfall, shielding her eyes against the sun to try and spot its source high up the mountain.

"Will this be all right?" Remick asked.

"For the picnic? It's perfect!"

He smiled, and shook the blanket out onto the ground.

"How did you find it?" Angie asked him. "How would you even know it was here?"

"I get about. I just came across it one day and thought it might make a good place to bring a beautiful woman for a picnic sometime."

"Have you brought many beautiful women here?"

"I haven't brought anyone, beautiful or otherwise. I haven't wanted to. Not until now."

"And I'm beautiful, am I?"

"You are the most beautiful woman I have ever seen. Now that's enough compliments. Let's eat."

"Oh I don't know," Angie said as she sat down on the blanket. "I don't think I could ever get enough compliments from you."

"You'll get them too, but for now, eat!"

Remick opened the hamper and took out a fresh selection of delicacies, all chosen to be as tempting as those he had brought the last time but with enough variety to stop Angie thinking he lacked imagination. Once again, she tucked in with relish.

After they had eaten, they lay back on the blanket side by side, hands touching, warming themselves and dozing in the sun, or at least, Angie dozed. Remick was not the dozing kind. Instead he lay there, enjoying the feel of Angie's hand and listening to her breathe.

Humans, he thought. They rarely appreciated the simple functions, the eating, the breathing. They took them for granted. But the pleasure with which Angie ate, the blissful smile on her face as she dozed and breathed, all made her feel so *alive* to him. It was a feeling he never wanted to let go and, lucky him, he had the ability to ensure he never had to. There were one or two things she would have to get used to, but she seemed an adaptable sort of person. She would, he hoped, understand the benefit of it in the end. Who wouldn't want to live forever?

Angie had been dozing for nearly an hour when she rolled onto her side and said, "You know what I want to do?"

"What's that?" Remick raised himself on one elbow to look at her.

"I want to get under that waterfall."

"You'll get your clothes wet."

"I won't be wearing any clothes. What do you think? You want to?"

So they did. Leaving their clothes on the blanket, they ran hand in hand to the waterfall. Angie shrieked as the cold mountain water hit her shoulders, but she would not come out. They stood in each other's arms as the torrent battered them and kissed as the water formed a seal between their bodies. Remick could almost believe the water made him feel cleansed.

Afterwards, they huddled together, still naked, with the blanket wrapped round them. Angie kissed him again, long and sweet, and he knew without question what she wanted.

"What if someone comes?" he asked.

"I'm counting on it."

Remick did not leave her that night, not exactly. When she invited him to stay, he readily agreed. Unbeknownst to her, he left her for a while as she slept to make his preparations for the following day, but he closed time around him so she never knew he was gone. There were things he had to do because as far as Angie knew, she was going to wake up on Monday, and Remick could not allow the day to end.

15.

B RIAN NORRIS LAY in the hospital bed, staring at the ceiling. Around him in the half-light which the hospital called night, machines attached to other patients bleeped and pinged. The nighttime meds they had tried to make him take had been concealed under his tongue and were now sticking his pillows together in a saliva-coated mass. He knew his clothes were in a locker beside his bed—he had checked several times. He just needed the opportunity.

It came when the basket-case in the bed at the end of the ward woke up from a nightmare screaming. The night staff hurried over to calm him down before he disturbed everybody, and as they did, Brian climbed out of bed on wobbly legs. One of the nurses spotted him and asked where he was going.

"Toilet," he replied, and the nurse, apparently satisfied, turned her attention back to Mr. Screamer. Brian quickly opened the locker, grabbed the carrier bag containing his clothes, and hurried to the patients' toilet at the end of the ward. By the time the other patient had been sedated and settled down, Brian was gone.

16.

I T WAS FAIRLY easy for Remick to make Angie believe she did not need to go into work the next day. Although he could still not see forwards in her timeline, he could see back and, after some searching, located the last time she had arranged some time off. It was a little more difficult than he had expected; for some reason, she rarely took holidays, but once he had located the memory, he was able to adapt it subtly and plant it back in her sleeping mind. He did not take the decision lightly. Normally, using his abilities in this way would not have given him any second thoughts at all, but he found himself reluctant to trick Angie. It was, however, necessary if he was to make this perfect summer last for her. He knew it had worked when she woke up and remarked that it was another beautiful day.

"Aren't you glad you booked the week off?" he asked.

"I know! Wasn't that lucky? Mind you, this time of year it can't last."

"We'll see," Remick said, knowing it could.

That day, they went to an outdoor cinema to see a film Remick thought she would like and spent the whole film kissing like teenagers. That evening, he cooked for her. It was the first meal he had ever cooked for anyone, but fortunately, he had been able to spend some time while Angie slept the previous night practising and perfecting a meal in the style of a chef whom he had found, while in Angie's memories, to be one of her favourites.

As they lay in bed that night, they made plans to visit a nearby stately home and have yet another picnic in its grounds. It surprised Remick that Angie wanted to go there, but she simply replied, "I like old things." That, Remick thought, was very lucky indeed.

The whole day was so perfect Remick never considered Brian Norris once. That was probably the biggest mistake that he had ever made in the whole of his long, long life.

17.

O N THE FOURTH day of summer, Brian Norris found them.
It had not been hard. He knew perfectly well where Angie
lived. Even though whenever they had spent the night together it
had always been at his flat, he had dropped her off at her building
many times. He preferred his flat to hers; his was bigger, more
expensive and furnished in the latest, minimalist style. Hers was
full of stuff, things scattered about at random, and if there was
one thing Brian Norris hated, it was mess.

After leaving the hospital, he had gone back to his flat,
which he was relieved to find was still there, just as he had left
it. He showered, changed and drove to Angie's street. He had
sat in his car, peering through the rain as it hammered down
on his windscreen, and waited for the morning, hoping to catch
Angie on her way to work. He badly needed to talk to her, to try
to explain what had happened to him. He was horrified when
the door to Angie's building opened and she came out dressed
bizarrely in a summer dress, accompanied by *him*, that creature,
whatever he was, the one who had done all this.

Before Brian could do anything, they had got into a car and
driven off. Angie had been laughing at something, clinging to
that monster's arm, walking through the rain to the car as if
she didn't feel the downpour at all. Brian watched the car turn
a corner and knew that his shocked indecision had cost him
the chance to follow. He had no idea where they were going, but
dressed like that, she certainly wasn't being given a lift to work.

He wondered at first whether to go to the police. But to say
what? They had not believed him in the hospital, and Angie

hardly seemed to be being held against her will. He resolved instead to wait. He was used to sorting out his own problems, and this would be no exception. He made a mental note of the make and registration number of the car the Devil was driving and sat in his own car all day with the rain pouring down the windows, awaiting its return.

It was early evening before the car came back. By then, Brian was cold, tired and hungry and all the more determined to let Angie know exactly who she was getting involved with, but when he saw the car draw up and Angie and the man who was not really a man get out, something happened which stopped him from acting. He suddenly felt, with a chilling clarity, the cold emptiness of the place this creature had sent him and remained frozen in his seat. He watched as Angie and that…*thing*, whatever it was…got out of the car and walked arm in arm to her building, looking like the rain did not touch them. He watched them go through the door and into the building, then waited some more to see if he/it would come out again. *This time*, Brian thought. This time he would get out of the car and put things right. But the door to the building did not open and remained closed all night.

He sat hunched over the steering wheel, fuming. Angie had clearly wasted no time. It had only been days since that bastard did whatever he had done. As the night dragged on, Brian thought more and more about what had happened to him. He was a rational man and did not believe in ghosts, UFOs or the Loch Ness Monster. He was not even sure he believed in God, and yet he had been prepared to believe that he had been attacked by the Devil.

He was now trying to come up with a rational explanation for what had happened, and all he could think of was that maybe his coffee had been drugged while he wasn't looking. Maybe that was why he had reacted so badly. That empty place was surely just a trick of some kind or a hallucination, and nobody's eyes burned like that…did they? But as soon as he was out of the way, Angie had obviously jumped straight into bed with the man. Or maybe she hadn't waited at all. Maybe it had been going on for a while, and what had happened to Brian was all part of it. Perhaps they were working together against him, Either way, as soon as they showed themselves in the morning, he intended to end it.

Brian assumed he'd fallen asleep at some point. One minute, he was squinting through the darkness and the driving rain at Angie's building, and the next, the sky was a murky, lighter grey and Brian was wiping a sticky tendril of drool from his chin. He briefly considered driving to the nearest McDonald's to grab some breakfast but thought better of it. It would be just his luck if he was delayed and could not get a parking space when he got back. The clock on his dashboard told him it was just gone six, so, assuming Angie was going to work, he would not have long to wait.

He must have dozed off again, because when the door to the building opened, the dashboard clock was showing eight-fifty. From what he knew of Angie's routine, it meant she was either running late, or not going into work at all.

She came out of the building wearing a summer dress again and sunglasses. *He* was in a T-shirt and jeans. They were dressed like it was the middle of the summer, and yet the rain which had been threatening for the last few hours had just started to fall. Neither of them seemed to notice. They kissed on the steps of the building and walked hand in hand to a nearby car. That was more than enough for Brian. He got out of his car and slammed the door shut.

18.

I T WAS THE slamming of the car door that alerted Remick. He looked over to see the source of the noise, and there was Brian Norris crossing the road towards them. Remick was incensed. *How dare he?* He let go of Angie's hand and stepped in front of her. He felt heat building up behind his eyes and did not want her to see.

"Good morning," he said, keeping his voice as light and controlled as he could. "Can I help?"

"You bastard," Brian spat. "What the hell did you do to me?"

"I don't know what you mean. Do to you? I haven't done anything to you. I'm sorry, but I don't even know who you are."

"You know damn well what you did. What was it? Acid? Roofies?" He turned to Angie. "Your boyfriend drugged me. He couldn't get you any other way, so he drugged me."

"I did nothing of the kind. We've never met before. Come on, Angie, let's go."

"Don't do it, Angie," Brian warned. "Don't go with him. You can't trust him."

"Look…" Remick tried to sound reasonable. "You and Angie clearly have some kind of history, but she's with me now. I suggest you let it go and leave us alone." He tried to turn his back on Brian, but the other man was not prepared to leave it there.

"He's lying, Angie. He knows damn well who I am. He followed me and drugged me and made me see things."

"Wait a minute," Angie said, speaking for the first time. "Stop it, both of you! I'm not going to have you arguing over me in the street like this. Let's talk about it like grown-ups, shall we?" Both men were shocked into silence. They looked at their feet, at the sky, anywhere but at each other or Angie, who had not finished yet. "When's Remy supposed to have done this, Brian? You can't just go round accusing people—"

"Couple of days ago. He turned up in that coffee shop and warned me off you. Told me to finish with you. When I wouldn't, he did…well, he did *something*. He put me in bloody hospital."

"That explains it," Remick said. "If you've just come out of hospital, that says it all. And it was a psychiatric ward, wasn't it, Brian?"

There was a long, stunned silence. Then Angie said, "Hang on. A psychiatric ward? Remy, how do you know that?" and Remick knew he had made a grave mistake.

19.

A NGIE HAD NO idea what was going on, but she did not like any of it. She had woken up that morning feeling great. Another gorgeous sunny day, and Remy had stayed with her, holding her all night. Then, suddenly, instead of taking her to the stately home he had promised, Remy was standing in the middle of the road arguing with her ex. What was worse, much worse, was that they sounded like they knew each other and Remy had lied.

"Remy," she asked again, "what the hell's going on?"

"Nothing's going on. I had a quick word with Brian here and suggested that he left you alone, that's all. All this stuff about drugs is nonsense."

"When?"

"When what?"

"When did you speak to him?"

Brian started to answer, but Angie held a hand up to caution him.

"*When*, Remy?"

"I'm not sure. I…"

"Let's see if we can narrow it down then. Was it before or after we started to go out?"

"I can't think. Does it matter? He's just trying to cause trouble. I think we should go."

"It matters to me. Was it before or after? And please don't lie to me."

Remy delayed long enough for Angie to know that the next thing that came out of his mouth might well not be the truth.

"Before."

"Right. I see." Angie turned away, her head reeling. This was obviously the truth, and it was all a bit too much to take in. "Look, sorry. I can't do this right now."

"I can explain…" Remy began.

"I don't want explanations. I don't know if I can trust them. You've already lied to me once. You pretended you didn't know Brian, and all the time, *all the time* we've been together, you knew what you'd done. I don't know if you did drug him or what, but you did *something*. I can't deal with this. Sort it out between you, but leave me out of it."

As she started up the steps, she heard Brian speak.

"Say what you like about me, but I never lied to her. I didn't have to trick her into bed…" Then his voice was cut off and he made a peculiar choking sound.

Angie looked back and her new boyfriend had her ex-boyfriend by the throat and had lifted him one-handed off his feet. For some reason, it was raining.

20.

THE ANGER WHICH had been building in Remick burst like a dam breaking. This pathetic mortal who had no more significance than an insect dared to challenge him? He felt the fire burning in his eyes and the glamour which kept him in his ridiculous human form began to slip, but he did not care. Angie was *his*. All he had done to win her, all the time and planning and love he had given to her and one stupid, short-lived gnat was going to ruin it for him.

His hand closed around Norris's throat. It would just take one squeeze and he could end it. No second chances, no taking him out of time, just the end of his tiny existence. Rain hissed and turned to steam as it hit him, and he flexed his muscles, ready for that one last, terminal squeeze.

But then Angie screamed, "NO! Remy, leave him!" and then, "Jesus Christ, what *are* you?" and that was that.

Summer was over.

21.

IN THE END, Remick could only do one thing. Instead of killing Norris—something he surely deserved—he erased all memory of the last few days from his mind and set a few fail-safes in there that would wipe his mind altogether should he try to remember. Then, as a last gift, he placed his hand on Angie's beautiful cheek even though she tried to shrink away from him.

He wiped her memories too, but without the fail-safes; that would be too cruel. As he did so, he knew why he had not been able to read her future. It was a future he would have no part of and did not want to see. He had hidden it from his own sight.

He looked at Angie for one last time, and then he walked away, leaving the two mortals standing bewildered in the rain outside Angie's building.

22.

H E NEVER TRIED to check on her, not in this world or any other. The thought that she might have returned to Norris or that she might just be getting on with her life without him was too much to bear. For a brief moment, Remick had known what it felt to love with all its joy and all its pain. He did not know how mortals went through their short, flickering lives doing it all the time. He just knew he never wanted to do it again. He was better off alone and would remain that way.

He took himself to a beach, but not the one he had been to with Angie. This was one guarded by a hundred iron statues who stood in the sand gazing blankly out to sea. It was a place Remick never visited because of the physical pain the element they were made of caused him. But it was a pain he wanted now, a pain he welcomed. All his powers had not been able to help him, and he wanted to be free of them. He trudged across the sand to the nearest of the iron men and placed both his hands on its head. He felt a wrench, like a million hooks tearing at his soul, and it was all he could do not to scream as his power, his very being, poured out into the metal. Then he slumped, spent, onto the sand and stayed there for a very long time.

It was night before Remick was able to heave himself to his feet. Unsteadily, he got up and started to walk back to the room he used, where he would stay for a very long time, drinking and dreaming of one perfect summer's day in winter which, like a flower growing out of season, bloomed gloriously and briefly but could never last.

About Seasons of Love

Love follows no rules. Like sun in winter and rain in summer, love can blossom in the most unexpected places. This richly diverse collection of stories proves that love is as universal and as varied as the seasons.

The Stories:

- *Tourist Season* – Deven Balsam
- *Machete Betty and the Office Sharks* – Neptune Flowers
- *Once Around Seven* – Ofelia Gränd
- *Winter Blossoms* – Paul Iasevoli
- *Year of the Guilty Soul* – A.M. Leibowitz
- *The Great Village Bun Fight* – Debbie McGowan
- *A Springful of Winters* – Dawn Sister
- *Out of Season* – Bob Stone
- *Seashell Voices* – Alexis Woods
- *Courting Light* – A. Zukowski

Available as a complete anthology (ebook/paperback)
and as individual stories (ebook + longer stories in paperback).

For more information/purchase links, visit:
www.beatentrackpublishing.com/SeasonsofLove

About Bob Stone

Liverpool born Bob Stone is an author and bookshop owner. He has been writing for as long as he could hold a pen and some would say his handwriting has never improved. He is the author of two self-published children's books, *A Bushy Tale* and *A Bushy Tale: The Brush Off*. *Missing Beat*, the first in a trilogy for Young Adults, is his first full-length novel.

Bob still lives in Liverpool with his wife and cat and sees no reason to change any of that.

By Bob Stone

Beaten Track Publishing

For more titles from Beaten Track Publishing,
please visit our website:

http://www.beatentrackpublishing.com

Thanks for reading!